THE BORLEY RECTORY
INCIDENT

TERRANCE DICKS

The
BORLEY
RECTORY
Incident

Piccadilly Press • London

The rights of Terrance Dicks and Andrew Skilleter to be
identified as Author and Cover illustrator of this work have
been asserted by them in accordance with the
Copyright, Designs and Patents Act 1988

Phototypeset from author's disk by Piccadilly Press.
Printed and bound by WBC, Bridgend,
for the publishers Piccadilly Press Ltd.,
5 Castle Road, London NW1 8PR

A catalogue record for this book is available from
the British Library

ISBNs: 1 85340 429 2 (trade paperback)
1 85340 535 3 (hardback)

Terrance Dicks lives in North London. He has written many books
for Piccadilly Press including the CHRONICLES OF A COMPUTER
GAME ADDICT series, the HARVEY series and THE GOOD, THE BAD
AND THE GHASTLY series.

Cover design by Judith Robertson

PROLOGUE

The minister awoke, shuddering with fear.

He was in a four-poster bed in the third-floor bedroom of his official residence, close to Hyde Park.

There seemed little for him to be frightened about.

He was one of the most powerful men in the country. He spent his days surrounded by comfort and luxury of every kind, by attentive secretaries and servants. Day and night he was surrounded by security men.

Armed police patrolled the gardens, front and back, and plainclothes bodyguards, also armed, were constantly on guard inside the house.

At that very moment a burly young man in a dark blue suit sat in a chair outside the minister's bedroom door.

The young man yawned a little, adjusted the

weight of the holstered 9mm automatic pistol under his arm, and looked forward to being relieved.

It was just before dawn.

Inside the bedroom a vase fell suddenly from the bedroom mantelpiece, shattering in the marble fireplace.

The minister sat bolt upright in bed, his eyes widening in terror.

The mirror over the mantelpiece shattered, suddenly, dropping into a thousand fragments on the hearth.

The minister screamed.

His bedroom door was flung open and the burly young man appeared, automatic in hand.

'Minister? Are you all right?'

The minister sprang from his bed and rushed towards him. 'Leave me alone!' he screamed. 'Get out of my way!'

The young man grabbed him. 'Minister, it's me, Wainwright. What's the matter?'

The minister threw him aside, sending him crashing into the corner of the room.

By now two more security men were crowding into the doorway.

'The minister's hysterical!' yelled Wainwright. 'Stop him!'

The little group of security men fanned out and advanced warily on the minister.

The minister, a slight, silver-haired figure in expensive silk pyjamas, stood, staring wild-eyed at them, trembling with fear.

Wainwright scrambled to his feet and joined his fellow security men. 'It's all right, minister,' he said soothingly. 'It's only us, nobody's going to hurt you.'

The little group closed in.

Suddenly the minister whirled round, dashed straight towards the closed French windows and hurled himself through them, ripping away the curtains and shattering both the glass and wooden framework.

Still entangled in the heavy curtains, the figure shot clean over the little balcony and smashed down on to the stone patio three storeys below.

There were shouts and yells from the garden and police began converging on the huddled, motionless form.

Wainwright went over to the window and

looked down for a moment. Then, ignoring his stunned colleagues, he went to the bedside phone, picked it up and dialled.

'Wainwright here, priority call for the director. Yes, I do know the time, thank you, wake her up! Tell her there's been another one . . .'

Chapter One

NIGHTMARE

I shrank back as the ghostly figure came out of the wall towards me. It was a big, red-faced man in the clothes of a nineteenth-century parson. He was clutching a riding-whip which he waved angrily at me.

'Who are you?' he bellowed. 'Why have you come here?'

An oil-lamp standing on a table suddenly flew through the air, hit the wall by the window and exploded, setting fire to long velvet curtains.

The ghostly giant ignored the blaze.

'Who are you, I say?'

'Matthew,' I croaked. 'My name is Matthew . . .'

'Matthew?' roared the angry giant. 'Matthew?'

'Matthew! Matthew! Wake up!'

I opened my eyes and realised that the hand shaking my shoulder and the voice calling my name belonged not to some angry ghost but to my father, Professor James Stirling.

I've never been more pleased to see him.

Not that he was a particularly pretty sight. He was perched on the side of my bed in baggy, nineteen-thirties-style striped pyjamas, his glasses askew on the end of his nose and his hair, what there is of it, sticking up all over the place.

'You've been having a nightmare, Matthew,' he announced unnecessarily. 'You were shouting and calling out. You made so much noise that you woke me up!'

Trust him to think of his own convenience first.

I sat up, rubbing my eyes. 'Sorry,' I said groggily. 'Haven't had a nightmare for years. Used to have them a lot when I was little. Used to sleepwalk as well.'

Dad seemed less than thrilled by this revelation. He's a selfish old devil, and he was probably wondering how many more interrupted nights lay ahead. 'Really?' he said. 'I didn't know that.'

'Well, you weren't there, were you?'

He didn't reply.

'Sorry,' I said. 'I didn't mean it to come out like that.'

We were on dodgy emotional ground here. My parents had separated, fairly amicably, when I was still a baby. Dad's a scientist, and in those days he had no time for anything except his work – come to think of it, he hasn't changed all that much.

Anyway, Mum decided she wanted a life of her own, and when Dad went off to work in America she stayed behind, and so did I. As I was still in nappies at the time I didn't really have much choice.

Mum did a pretty good job of bringing me up alone – until she was killed in a car crash when I was twelve. After that her sister Ellen took over the job. Three years later Jim, Ellen's husband, took early retirement and they went to live in Spain.

Suddenly Dad found himself with a completely unknown son on his hands.

As if this wasn't enough trouble, his research funds (Dad's one of the world's top space scientists) suddenly dried up at the same time. Luckily – although he didn't exactly see it that way – he was offered another job almost immediately.

An American scientific research institute

needed a distinguished scientist to head its newly established Department of Paranormal Studies, founded as a result of a bequest from an eccentric millionaire.

Dad's attitude to the paranormal is sceptical to say the least. Nevertheless, he decided to solve two problems at once, by accepting the job and taking me on as his assistant. He took me out of school and announced he was taking over my education himself. He's got degrees in practically everything, so nobody argued.

As far as Dad's concerned, paranormal research is a stopgap until the US Government comes to its senses, sets up a new space programme with him in charge, and starts building rockets to go to Mars.

However, the job does have its advantages, including a massive salary and apparently unlimited expenses. Dad's a conscientious character and, despite his doubts, he takes the job very seriously. Already we'd worked on a number of investigations as far afield as the Australian outback and the Bermuda Triangle, and as close to home as Stonehenge.

We'd had some uncanny experiences that had

shaken Dad's scepticism considerably – not that he'd ever admit it, of course.

At the moment we were back in our top-floor Hampstead flat looking, though not too hard, for another project and enjoying a period of peaceful research.

Peaceful, that is, until my sudden nightmare.

There was an awkward silence after my unfortunate remark.

Then Dad said, 'I can't pretend to offer the kind of comfort your mother would have done . . .'

I grinned. 'She used to let me get in bed with her and give me a cuddle. I don't think we'll bother, thanks.'

Ignoring the interruption, Dad said, 'However, if you would like me to sit with you for a while . . .'

I shook my head. 'No need, thanks all the same. I'll get up and make a cup of tea and then try to get back to sleep. Want one?'

'Thank you, no.' Dad got up, then hesitated in the doorway. 'I shouldn't let it worry you too much, Matthew,' he said. 'Your nightmare, I mean. The kind of work we've been doing is bound to take its toll.'

I nodded. 'I suppose so. But the funny thing is, it wasn't anything like what we've been dealing with recently. My nightmare, I mean. No aliens or UFOs or anything like that.'

'So what was it about?'

'More like a mixed-up version of your traditional ghost story. Dark old house, ghosts, things flying through the air . . .'

'As in poltergeist activity?'

'Yes, I suppose so.'

'Interesting,' said Dad. 'Poltergeists, you know, are probably the most commonly reported and the best documented paranormal phenomena of all. Maybe we should consider making them our next project.' He yawned. 'Oh well, we can talk about it tomorrow. Good night, Matthew.'

He cleared off to bed and after a bit I got up and went into our super-modern kitchen and made a cup of tea. There's something very comforting about modern kitchen appliances and neon lighting.

I sat, sipping tea and thinking about my dream . . .

I pushed open the creaking door and went inside. There

was a heavy iron stove just in front of me and a flight of stairs leading upwards. Suddenly a red glass candlestick came whizzing down the stairs and shattered against the stove . . .

I jumped at the sound of breaking glass and found myself back at the kitchen table.

My mug had rolled off the table and smashed on the floor. It wasn't exactly Hammer Horror, but it was more than enough to make me jump.

I nearly yelled for Dad but I decided he wouldn't appreciate losing more sleep over one smashed mug.

I shook my head and rubbed my eyes. It wasn't just that I'd *remembered* my dream. For a moment there I'd been back inside it. Far from being forgotten, the nightmare had returned with renewed force.

What was going on?

I stood up and went over to the window.

Although things were brightly lit inside, everything was very dark and mysterious outside. Our flat is on the top floor of a block that overlooks the heath. It was a wild, wet night and through the big windows I could see storm-tossed treetops and the surrounding darkness of the open heath.

Letters suddenly appeared on the wall. Straggling red letters, apparently written in blood:

DANGER! BEWARE! TURN BACK!

Then another message scrawled below:

HELP ME! PLEASE HELP ME!

I looked up and saw a shadowy, hooded figure. It was a nun. She moved slowly away, disappearing through the wall . . .

I jumped back from the window. It had happened again! I was wide awake – but at the same time, I was back in the dream.

I struggled to remember more details about my nightmare.

It had been a sort of supernatural supermarket, something of everything. Phantom nuns, ghostly vicars, mysterious writing, things flying through the air . . .

The odd thing was that it all seemed strangely familiar somehow. Perhaps it was just a confused rehash of things I'd seen and read. Old horror movies, ghost stories, fragments of research. But somehow there was more to it than that.

The old house in the dream seemed as familiar as all the strange things that had happened there. Surely so many supernatural events could never have happened in just one place?

Suddenly it came to me.

Borley Rectory! The most haunted house in England.

I was pretty sure that all the things I'd seen and a lot more as well would have been reported as occurring at Borley Rectory.

But why should I dream about the place?

I'd never been there. There was no longer any rectory to visit, the place had burned down years ago. I'd never studied the place particularly, just picked up a few of the basic facts somewhere. Borley Rectory had been a supernatural superstar in the twenties and thirties, with even more journalists, mediums and psychic investigators than ghosts infesting the place.

After the mysterious fire, which had happened

just before the war, interest had naturally died down.

But the details would be on the Internet – and in all the reference books. I went into my little study.

I couldn't get a connection to the Net, so I began looking through the extensive paranormal library that I'd bought with the institute's funds.

I soon found what I was looking for. Borley Rectory featured in most of the reference books and so did all the phenomena I'd seen in my dream – flying candlesticks and a variety of other objects, ghostly nun and vicar, messages written in blood on the walls, mysterious fires – the lot had been reported at Borley Rectory.

In one account, the story of a visit to Borley Rectory by one of the many researchers who'd studied the place, I found rather more than I'd expected.

The researcher had noticed 'a pair of very nice red glass candlesticks' in one of the most haunted rooms. As he was coming down the stairs with a companion, '. . . one of those nice red candlesticks hurtled down the stairs, hit the iron stove in the hall and disintegrated into a thousand fragments.'

I remembered the iron stove in the hall and the red glass candlestick flying past my head.

I had been to Borley Rectory in my dream.

To a place which no longer existed.

Closing the book, I went back into the kitchen.

What is going on? I wondered.

I wasn't just dreaming about Borley Rectory. I was being haunted by it!

I picked up the pieces of smashed mug, put them in the rubbish bin and went back to bed.

It took me a long time to get to sleep. And when I did . . .

I was standing in the middle of a cluttered Victorian sitting-room.

Suddenly I heard the sound of a stagecoach approaching the house. I could hear the pounding of the horses' hooves, the jingling of the harness, the creaking of the heavy wooden coach.

I ran to the window and looked out. In the bright moonlight I could see the road running past the house. I could hear the ghostly stagecoach rattling past the house, but I couldn't see it. The lonely country road was empty and deserted. I turned back into the room.

There was a bell-rope hanging by the fireplace. It started lashing to and fro like an angry snake. Somewhere in the house a bell jangled, then another, and another. The air was filled with the sound of bells . . .

I opened my eyes to find myself tucked up in bed – with my bedside alarm-clock jangling.

I switched it off and turned over, hoping to get back to sleep.

Some hopes.

I was just drifting away again when Dad rushed into my room. 'Wake up, Matthew! Wake up!'

'Why? Are you having nightmares?'

'We've been summoned by Security,' announced Dad importantly. 'Our old friend Ms Alexander.'

I struggled to wake up. 'Why? What about?'

'Mysterious death of a minister. As Sherlock Holmes used to say, "the police are baffled." '

'Why involve us?'

'Because there appears to be evidence of poltergeist activity. Quite a coincidence, don't you think, Matthew?'

As I fought my way into my clothes, I thought of my disturbed night and my nightmare.

I wondered how much of a coincidence it really was . . .

Chapter Two

CRIME SCENE

They'd taken the minister away by the time we arrived.

As I looked through the broken window I wasn't sorry. After a fall like that he couldn't have been a pretty sight.

All that was left was the chalk outline of a body on the paving stones below.

'He died instantly,' said Chief Inspector Blane. 'No problems about how. What's baffling us all is why!'

Blane, like Ms Alexander, was an old acquaintance. We'd met them both on the Stonehenge business. Chief Inspector Blane was Special Branch, inevitably called in when the 'funnies' – the regular police's not-too-affectionate nickname for the Intelligence Services – were involved. He was the same as ever: tall, dark and serious in a black trench-coat.

Ms Alexander hadn't changed either. Neat, trim and composed, in a smart suit and serious glasses, she was the picture of the woman who has made it big in business. She didn't look like a top spy, more like someone who ran a firm of stockbrokers or a bank.

Beside her stood a very large, tough-looking young man in a rumpled dark blue suit. He looked tired, as if he'd been up all night.

Ms Alexander introduced him. 'This is James Wainwright, in charge of the minister's body-guard squad.'

Wainwright looked worried as well as tired – natural enough, since the minister he'd been bodyguarding had ended up on the paving stones below.

'This is Professor James Stirling and his son – and assistant – Matthew Stirling,' Ms Alexander went on. 'They've been called in as specialist consultants.'

She didn't say what we were specialists in, which was probably just as well.

As usual, Dad lost no time in taking over.

'I'd be grateful if you could give me a full account of what happened,' he said crisply. 'In as much detail as possible, please.'

Wainwright looked at Ms Alexander and she nodded. 'Go ahead, Mr Wainwright. Professor Stirling has full security clearance.'

Next Wainwright gave *me* a worried look.

'My assistant has the same security clearance as I do myself,' snapped Dad. 'Now, if we could get on?'

Wainwright looked again at Ms Alexander and she nodded in confirmation.

He gave me an apologetic look. 'Sorry, force of habit.'

' "I'm a professional," ' I quoted. ' "I wouldn't tell my own mother where I keep the fuse wire." '

Wainwright looked baffled for a moment and then grinned. 'Len Deighton, right? *The Ipcress File.*'

'I think so,' I said. 'Or is it *Billion Dollar Brain*?'

Dad doesn't care for spy novels and he hates being upstaged. 'If we could postpone the literary discussions until later?'

'Sorry, professor,' said Wainwright solemnly. He gave me a quick, amused glance and I could see he had Dad's number.

He began his story. 'It was just before dawn. I took the last night shift myself. There are six of us; we work four-hour shifts.'

Dad nodded. 'And you were where?'

'In a chair outside the door. Two of the others were checking the house; the other three were asleep. There were armed police patrols all round the house.'

'That's a lot of security,' said Dad. 'Is that routine, or was there some special reason?'

Wainwright flicked a quick glance at Ms Alexander who said smoothly, 'He *was* a minister, you know. And in the current political situation . . .'

She's lying, I thought. Lying expertly, but still lying.

Wainwright went on with his tale. 'First thing I heard was the sound of something breaking. It wasn't very loud – might have been a cup or a vase or something.'

Chief Inspector Blane went over to the fireplace. The hearth was filled with shattered pieces of mirror and there was a blank space above the mantelpiece where the mirror had been. He stooped and examined the mess for a moment, took a silver pencil from his pocket and poked around in the glittering shards of mirror. Then he reached out and picked up a piece of blue and white china. He straightened up, holding it out.

'This matches that Chinese vase still on the mantelpiece. There are other fragments, mixed in beneath the broken glass.'

'Which suggests that the first noise you heard, Mr Wainwright, was the vase falling from the mantelpiece,' said Dad. 'Why?'

Wainwright shrugged. 'No idea.'

'Was it windy? Was the window open?'

'No to both,' said Wainwright. 'It was a still night and the window was shut; the minister hated draughts.'

Dad nodded. 'Go on.'

'I thought the minister must have knocked over his water glass or something, but I decided I'd better check. Just as I stood up I heard the most almighty crash – I suppose it must have been the mirror going – then the minister screamed. By this time I was on my way into the bedroom. The mirror was smashed and the minister was sitting up in bed looking terrified.'

'And there was nobody else there? No way anyone could have just left?'

Wainwright shook his head. 'Definitely not. As you can see, there are no other exits.'

'Could anyone have been hiding in here?' asked Dad.

'I doubt it. We checked – afterwards – and there was nobody. Besides, the room was under constant guard: no way they could have got in or out.'

'Sorry to interrupt,' said Dad. 'Please go on.'

'When he saw me, the minister jumped out of bed. He seemed terrified – he was even frightened of *me*! I said something like, "Don't worry, it's only me," but he rushed at me. I could see he was hysterical so I tried to grab him.'

'Tried?'

'He just threw me aside.'

Dad studied him and frowned. 'Was the minister a large man?'

'The minister,' said Ms Alexander, 'was of average height, thin and rather frail. He was also sixty-two years old.'

Dad looked at Wainwright and raised an eyebrow.

'I know,' said Wainwright helplessly. 'I'm six foot two, I weigh fifteen stone and I'm SAS trained. He picked me up and chucked me in the corner of the room.'

There was a little silence.

I was getting fed up with keeping quiet. 'I saw this TV documentary ages ago,' I said diffidently, 'about an English policeman who joined the cops in Los Angeles . . .'

Everyone looked at me as if I'd gone potty.

Dad said, 'Really, Matthew . . .'

Having started, I carried on regardless. '. . . He told this story about trying to arrest a little old lady who was out of her head on crack cocaine. She picked him up and threw him through a plate-glass window. He was quite a big chap as well.'

Ms Alexander gave me an icy glare. 'If you're suggesting that the minister was on drugs . . .'

'I'm only suggesting he was in an abnormal mental state,' I said. 'And abnormal mental states can produce physical reactions – like abnormal strength.'

'I'm sorry, Mr Wainwright,' said Dad. 'Do continue.'

'There's not much more left to tell. The other two bodyguards had heard the racket and they all turned up, more or less at once. I picked myself up and we all four closed in on him. Maybe it was a mistake. It seemed to panic him even more. Suddenly he whirled round and hurled himself through the window.'

'Ripping away a heavy velvet curtain and smashing through a pretty solid wooden window-frame,' said Chief Inspector Blane.

He looked at me. 'Which seems to bear out your abnormal physical strength theory, Matthew.'

Ms Alexander turned to Dad. 'Well, that's the full story, Professor Stirling. Is it too soon to ask what you make of it?'

To my utter amazement Dad said, 'Well, to begin with, there seems to be clear indications of poltergeist activity . . .'

Wainwright gaped at him. 'Poltergeists? You mean ghosts? Spooks?'

A sceptic himself, Dad hates not being taken seriously. 'I assure you, Mr Wainwright, that if any aspect of the paranormal can be considered scientifically proven, it is poltergeist activity. There are hundreds, indeed thousands of well-authenticated cases.'

Wainwright shook his head in disbelief. I could hardly blame him. James Bond never had to cope with this sort of thing. And what use was a Walther PPK against a ghost?

He looked appealingly at Ms Alexander, clearly wondering if he was supposed to take all this seriously.

'Perhaps I should have explained, Mr Wainwright,' she said. 'Professor Stirling is head of the Scientific Research Institute's Department of Paranormal Studies.'

Which was, if anything, an understatement. Dad pretty well *was* the Department of Paranormal Studies – along with me, of course.

Dad gave Wainwright a satirical look. 'Don't worry, Mr Wainwright, we're the last resort. Like calling in a psychic or a gipsy fortune-teller when all else fails. You must admit that what's happened here is pretty hard to explain.'

Wainwright nodded. 'All the same . . . No disrespect, professor, but – ghosts!'

'Not necessarily. There could be a scientific explanation.'

'But you said . . . '

I could see Dad starting to simmer, so I

hurriedly jumped in. 'There are two theories about poltergeists, Mr Wainwright. One is the supernatural one, that they're mischievous evil spirits or angry ghosts. The other, the more scientific one, is that poltergeist-type effects are caused by telekinetic energy, produced by the human brain.'

I could see by Dad's expression that he wasn't too pleased at losing the floor, and added, 'That is right, isn't it, Dad?'

'Exactly so,' he said. 'In the vast majority of cases there is an unhappy or disturbed adolescent on the premises, usually a teenage girl. Is there anyone in this house who fits that description?'

Ms Alexander looked at Wainwright enquiringly. He shook his head. 'This house is inhabited by civil servants, security men and domestic staff. I don't know if any of them are disturbed, but I'm damned sure none of them are adolescents.'

'No upstairs maids sobbing in the attics or unhappy bootboys in the basement?'

Dad's ideas about domestic service are rather Victorian.

'No!' said Wainwright. 'The cook and the domestic staff are all ladies of mature years.'

I spoke up once again. 'What about all the other cases?' I asked. 'Any unhappy adolescents involved there?'

There was a sudden silence.

Then Ms Alexander said icily, 'And who told you there were other cases?'

It was only a guess, but I was pleased to have it confirmed.

'As Dad said just now, we're the last resort. I don't think you'd have called us in over just *one* suspicious death.'

'I have to agree,' said Dad. 'What's more, I can't believe that this degree of security is routine, even for a minister. Armed police around the house and twenty-four-hour bodyguard coverage . . .'

'What are you suggesting?' asked Ms Alexander.

Well, I've gone this far, I thought . . . 'That you expected something to happen and were trying to protect the minister.'

It was obvious from her silence that I'd hit on the truth.

It was obvious to Dad as well. Typically, he blew his top.

'Do you mean that there have been a number of these incidents, and you have only just called us in? And then you have the impertinence to expect us to help you even though you are concealing the full facts?'

'I don't care for your tone, Professor Stirling,' said Ms Alexander freezingly. 'In Security, we operate on a strict need-to-know basis.'

Dad drew himself up to his full, considerable height. 'I, madam, am a research scientist, not a spy,' he thundered. 'And what I need to know is – *everything*!'

Two formidable personalities, they stood glaring at each other, she up, he down.

Nobody else said a word. Nobody dared.

Finally I drew a deep breath and broke the silence – I had nothing to lose.

'All right, Dad, come off your high horse. Ms Alexander has a lot of responsibility and she has to be careful.' I turned to Ms Alexander. 'All the same, Dad's right, you know. You have to trust us completely, or not at all. We need all the facts, the full picture, if we're going to help.'

There was another long, tense silence, then Ms Alexander said, 'You have a gift of diplomacy beyond your years, Matthew.' She turned to Dad. 'Of course I trust you, Professor Stirling. I simply wanted to see what you made of this case before telling you of the others.' She paused. 'Possibly that may have been a mistake.'

Dad cleared his throat. 'I see. Well, perhaps I spoke somewhat intemperately . . .'

It was as close to apologising as either of them could get and it was time to move things on.

'How bad is it?' I asked.

Ms Alexander said, 'There have been about a dozen cases in the last six months, all involving people of some importance – senior politicians, scientists, top civil servants. Some have committed suicide; the rest had complete breakdowns. If this goes on the country will be crippled – and we have no idea what to do. As you said, professor, you two are our last hope.'

A cold winter wind came into the room. I looked at the broken window and shuddered, wondering what terrible fear had driven a power-ful, successful, well-guarded man to hurl himself to his death.

The references to poltergeists and death had made me think of my nightmare about Borley

Rectory. Was it sheer coincidence, or was it possible that the mysterious deaths could be related to my nightmare?

I was soon to find out . . .

Chapter Three

THE SURVIVOR

'With the greatest possible respect, director, I think this is a grave mistake. To bring in outsiders in this way is quite unprecedented.'

The speaker was a tall, bald, bespectacled bureaucrat called Harker, who seemed to be Ms Alexander's second-in-command.

We were in a small but luxurious conference room at the top of an ultra-modern tower building beside the Thames, the HQ of Ms Alexander's mysterious Intelligence Department. Harker was clutching an armful of buff-coloured files, as if prepared to defend them with his life.

Ms Alexander gave him her well-known steely glare. 'Mistaken or not, the decision is mine, *deputy* director, and I have taken it. May I remind you that Professor Stirling and his son are not exactly outsiders? They gave considerable assistance to this department in the recent Stonehenge affair. And before that they aided our American colleagues in the Bermuda Triangle incident.'

Harker rubbed the back of his neck in nervous irritation. 'That's as may be, director. But in this case we are not dealing with flying saucers and little green men, but with a plot by enemy agents to destabilise the country.'

'We are not sure what we are dealing with, Mr Harker,' said Ms Alexander. 'That is precisely why we have called in Matthew and Professor Stirling. Leave the files, please – and ask them to send in some coffee and sandwiches. I hope you don't mind a working lunch, gentlemen?'

Dismissed, Harker put down the files and left in offended silence.

'I must apologise for my colleague,' said Ms Alexander. 'He's an excellent administrator, but unreceptive to new ideas.'

She smiled grimly. 'What's more, he thought he was in line for the post of director . . .' She got up. 'If you'll excuse me, I'll leave you to it.'

Fortified by coffee and sandwiches, Dad and I spent the next hour going through the files. They told an extraordinary tale.

Over the past six months, eleven VIPs had suffered sudden, shattering nervous breakdowns. The minister this morning brought the number up to twelve. Quite a few of them had attempted suicide – and six of them had succeeded. Seven if you counted the minister. The rest had cracked up completely, often attacking colleagues or friends. The survivors were still hospitalised. With one exception they were severely deranged, occasionally violent, and completely unfit for work.

We were reading the last files when Ms Alexander came back into the room.

'Any progress?'

Dad shook his head. 'I'm afraid not. I was looking for some kind of pattern . . .'

'And?'

'There doesn't seem to be one – apart from the obvious, that is. They were all engaged on work of national importance and they were all distinguished in their respective fields. They all held senior posts and were probably all working too hard. One might reasonably expect one or two to crack up. But so many, so quickly, and all in such a very short space of time . . . well, that's another matter entirely.'

I quoted one of my favourite sayings, 'Once is happenstance, twice is coincidence, three times is enemy action!'

'Who said that?' demanded Dad.

'Goldfinger – you know, James Bond's old mate. In the book, not the movie.'

Dad frowned. 'Really, Matthew, your taste in literature . . .'

Ms Alexander smiled. 'I like a good spy thriller myself. And there's something in what you say. Twelve times is most certainly enemy action. But what enemy? And how are they doing it?'

'Is this happening anywhere else?' asked Dad.

'Not as far as we know. We've made discreet enquiries, but no other country is having quite the same problem.'

'Perhaps it's a pilot scheme,' I said. 'If it works here, they'll try it all over the world.'

Ms Alexander shuddered. 'What a ghastly idea!'

'Britain's the ideal testing ground,' said Dad. 'A small, compact country . . . By neutralising a few top people you could paralyse the place!'

'Actually, I'm not so sure you're right about that,' I said.

Dad looked outraged. He's always sure he's right about everything, and hates anyone telling him he's not. Especially me . . .

'Indeed, Matthew?'

'Well, Britain isn't paralysed, is it?' I said.

'Not yet it isn't,' said Ms Alexander. 'But if this sort of thing goes on . . .'

I waved towards the pile of buff files. 'I suppose all these people have already been replaced – in whatever jobs they were doing?'

'I imagine so.'

'And you could replace a lot more like them, if you had to?'

'I suppose we could. What's your point?'

'It just doesn't seem to be a very effective sort of attack. They haven't gone for any really top people, like the Prime Minister or the Queen. And even if they did . . . *Nobody*'s indispensable, *anyone* can be replaced. They'd have to knock out hundreds, even thousands of people to have any real effect. It just doesn't seem worth the effort.'

'So what are you suggesting?'

'I'm not sure. It's just that there may be more

to this scheme than we realise.'

Dad gave me an impatient look, and I didn't really blame him. I didn't have a proper theory yet, just a vague feeling somewhere at the back of my mind.

Ms Alexander gave me a dismissive glance. 'Very interesting, Matthew,' she said, meaning the exact opposite.

She turned hopefully to Dad. 'Have *you* any suggestions to offer, Professor Stirling?'

'I should like to interview one of the survivors.'

'Anyone in particular?'

'Yes, this one.' Dad picked up a file. 'Doctor Backman; he's a research physicist. According to the file, he's recovering rather better than most of the others. I happen to know him slightly; perhaps I can persuade him to talk to me.'

'I'll arrange it right away. He's in a private hospital not far from here, one of our own places. Anything else?'

'Well, I've got an idea,' I said.

Dad and Ms Alexander exchanged tolerantly weary glances.

Ms Alexander decided she might as well

humour me. 'Well, Matthew?'

'I take it everything in these files is on computer?'

'Everything you've seen and a great deal more. Those particular files are only summaries. We did a very full background investigation into every case.'

'I think it might be worth your while to put someone on to reviewing all the material.'

She frowned. 'Why? What for?'

'To look for links.'

'What kind of links?'

'*Any* kind of links,' I said desperately. 'Anything a significant number of them have in common. Romanian grandmothers, yachting, stamp collecting, line dancing – anything at all.'

'Very well,' said Ms Alexander resignedly. 'I'll put Harker on to it.'

'No!' I said instinctively.

'I'm sorry?'

'Harker doesn't like us. He's likely to drag his feet.' I gave her my most appealing smile. 'Isn't there someone else? Someone young and keen?'

She considered for a moment. 'Young Wainwright, then. He's out of a job for the moment, with no minister to guard.'

She took a leather case from her pocket and gave us each a small white card, blank except for a telephone number.

'This telephone number is manned around the clock. If you need anything at all, equipment, support, anything, just call.' She looked at Dad and then at me, her face grave. 'I'm relying on you both to come up with something. In a way, I agree with you, Matthew. My instinct tells me we're looking at the tip of a very large and nasty iceberg.'

I nodded. 'And we all know what happened to the *Titanic* . . .'

'I don't know,' said Dr Backman hopelessly. 'I just don't know what happened to me . . .'

We were sitting in a pleasant bed-sitting-room with a view of a flower-garden outside. But the window was barred, and I knew that a thick-set man in a white coat stood outside the door.

We'd had quite a job persuading him to let us talk to Dr Backman alone.

Looking round I saw that there was nothing hard or heavy in the room, nothing that could be thrown or used as a weapon. The tables and chairs, even the bed, were fixed to the floor.

It was a high-class padded cell.

Dr Backman was a scrawny, nervous-looking type with rimless glasses and thinning fair hair. He seemed rational enough in a vague sort of way and he'd even seemed to recognise Dad. But there was a haggard, haunted look about him – not surprising in view of what had happened to him.

But then what had happened to him? He didn't seem able to tell us much.

'One moment I was working in my lab, writing up the notes of an experiment – then I woke up in here.'

He laughed nervously. 'They tell me I wrecked my own laboratory and half-throttled one of my colleagues – but I don't remember anything about it.'

'Had you been overworking?' asked Dad. 'Were you under some kind of exceptional strain?'

Dr Backman considered. 'Well, there's always some. I'm the head of a department engaged in an important weapons-research project. But I don't think I was any more stressed-out than usual. As a matter of fact, I'd just had a few days away.'

'Any particular reason?' I asked.

He shrugged. 'I think I just felt I needed a break.'

'Did the holiday help?'

'Not really. After I got back I started sleeping badly. I had nightmares . . .'

I felt a sudden chill.

I was climbing the stairs in an old, dark house. Climbing towards some unimaginable horror . . .

Heavy, dragging footsteps climbed the wooden stairs behind me. I turned but there was nobody there . . .

I came to a door at the top of the stairs. There was a heavy, old-fashioned key in the lock. I reached for the brass doorknob to see if the door was locked. Before my hand touched it, the key shot out of the lock and clattered on to the wooden floorboards . . .

'Matthew!' said Dad sharply. 'Matthew, are you all right?'

With an effort I wrenched myself back to the present. 'What sort of nightmares?' I asked. 'Ghosts?'

Dr Backman's eyes widened and he stared

fixedly at me. 'Yes, ghosts . . . There was a recurring nightmare . . .'

'Can you remember what it was about?'

His eyes grew even wider. 'I went through this big, heavy door, into the hall of an old, dark house.'

'Was there anything in the hall?'

'A stove . . . there was an old-fashioned iron stove.'

'What happened then? Did you go upstairs?'

'Yes . . . yes I did.' He ran his fingers through his straggly hair and rubbed the back of his neck.

'Did you see anyone?'

'There was a shape at the top of the stairs – a nun, I think. She vanished, went right through the wall . . .'

'Anything else?'

'There was writing . . . writing in letters of blood on the wall. "Help me!" I didn't want to go upstairs but I had to . . .'

'Matthew,' began Dad.

I waved him to silence, leaning forward to Dr Backman. I knew the colour had gone from my face, but I had to see how close his dream was to mine. 'What next?' I asked urgently. 'Did you see anything odd when you reached the door at the top of the stairs?'

'The key . . . it jumped out of the lock at me!'

'Did you hear anything strange?'

'There was a stagecoach,' he whispered. 'It went right past the house. I ran to the window but I couldn't see it!'

'Anything else?'

'Candlesticks. One of them flew through the air and smashed against the wall.'

'What were the candlesticks like?'

'They were made of glass . . .'

'Red glass?'

'That's right!' he gasped. 'Red glass! How did you know?'

'Did you see anything else? Did you see a ghost?'

Dr Backman sprang to his feet. 'He came through the wall! He tried to kill me! You all want to kill me!'

There was a bunch of chrysanthemums in a light plastic vase on the mantelpiece. Suddenly the vase flew across the room, hitting the opposite wall and scattering water and flowers across the carpet.

Instinctively I turned to look, which was a bad mistake. With a scream of rage Dr Backman hurled himself at my throat.

As his bony fingers closed round my neck I yelled as loud as I could, clasped my hands together and swung them upwards, breaking his grip.

He reached out again, but by this time Dad was on his back, trying to pull him off.

Backman twisted round, grabbed Dad and threw him across the room. (Luckily for Dad he landed on the bed.) Then he turned his attention back to me, claw-like hands reaching out . . .

By this time an alarm-bell was clanging and the man in the white coat was coming through the door, two others close behind him. It took all three of them to subdue Dr Backman . . .

Not long after that we were in a taxi heading back to Hampstead. We'd made a hasty retreat from the hospital, apologising to the white-coated attendant for ignoring his advice and apologising to the resident doctor for upsetting his prize patient.

I'd enquired if they'd noticed any mysterious

flying objects since Dr Backman had been with them, a question which earned me some rather strange looks. One of the attendants grudgingly admitted that they'd sometimes found the room trashed when Backman was particularly ill. They'd just assumed he'd done it himself.

I was quiet and subdued on the journey home. I'd been badly shaken by what had happened at the hospital – and not just by Dr Backman doing his best to throttle me either.

What was really terrifying was the way his nightmare seemed to be linked to mine.

What was happening to me? Was it possible that I could have the same 'illness' as Dr Backman? Would I go mad like him and the others?

Dad was in a grim and grumpy mood. He had yet to make the connections I was making about the dream and I was too terrified to acknowledge them myself.

'You realise how much we've set back poor Backman's recovery?'

'I know. I'm sorry – but I think it may have been necessary.'

'Why? What possessed you to ask those ridiculous questions?'

'When he talked about bad dreams I had a flashback to my nightmare last night. And the questions weren't so ridiculous either. They've given us our only clue so far.'

'What clue? What possible good did it do reminding that poor man of his nightmares? All you did was trigger an outburst of paranoid rage.'

'You still don't realise, do you, Dad?' I said desperately. 'His nightmare was my nightmare.'

'What on earth are you talking about, Matthew? Have you gone out of your mind?'

'No, but I might do at any moment. You'd better watch out!'

'Matthew!'

'Dr Backman and I have got something in common,' I said seriously. 'We have both been visiting Borley Rectory in our dreams.'

It took a lot of talking to convince Dad there was something in what I was saying.

Back in the flat I gave him a full account of my nightmare. I told him how closely the various Borley Rectory accounts corresponded to my dream.

I reminded him of what Backman had said

about *his* nightmare – and how that linked up to mine and the Borley Rectory references.

Naturally Dad had to play the sceptic. 'You could have picked up all that Borley Rectory stuff during your research,' he argued. 'It's just standard spooky stuff after all. Phantom nuns, invisible stagecoaches . . . Hardly surprising it should turn up in your nightmare.'

'I could have picked it up reading, but I didn't,' I said. 'Before last night I knew none of the *details* about the Borley hauntings. I just knew the "most haunted house in England" bit, nothing about red glass candlesticks and keys jumping out of locks. I looked all that up *after* the nightmare.'

Dad still wouldn't give up. 'Leaving that aside, you fed most of the Borley Rectory stuff to Backman in your questions. He just played it back.'

'Oh no I didn't!' I said, feeling like someone in a pantomime. 'I was very careful about that. I may have given him the cues, but he came up with the nun, the key, the writing in blood, the stagecoach and the red glass candlesticks all by himself.'

One of the many attributes of Dad's giant

brain is the power of total recall. He sat there for a moment, playing back his mental recording of my conversation with Dr Backman.

At last he nodded. 'You're quite right, Matthew. So, what do we do now?'

'We go down to Borley Rectory,' I said. 'What else can we do? I agree it's not much of a lead, but it's the only one we've got!'

'How can we go there?' snapped Dad. He tapped the pile of reference books. 'According to all these, the place burned down in 1939.' He flicked through one of the books. 'It's described here as "a rather unpicturesque ruin"!'

'Then we visit the village,' I said. 'Or just the general area. There's some kind of local link, there must be!'

It was my phone call to Ms Alexander's outfit that finally convinced him. I called the mystery number and managed to get put through to Wainwright.

'I gather you're the one I've got to thank for all these happy hours in front of the computer,' he said with mock bitterness. At least, I hoped it was mock.

'Sorry,' I said. 'Has it done any good? Have

you found any significant links between our victims yet?'

'Not a thing.'

'Can you try something for me?'

'Such as?'

'Have you got some kind of sort program?'

'Sure. We're all hi tech here. Fire away.'

'Try Borley Rectory,' I said.

There was a longish silence. Then his voice came back. 'Sorry, nothing.'

I suddenly remembered something Dr Backman had said. 'Try "break", or "holiday" or "weekend away" – and cross-reference with "Essex".'

There was another, longer pause. Then his excited voice said, 'Bingo! Every single one of them had a short holiday just before they cracked up. All the holidays were close to London – in either Essex or Suffolk.'

I felt a sudden pang of terror, and the image of a solid old Victorian building came into my mind.

Borley Rectory is – was – close to the Essex/Suffolk border.

I was going through a creaking door into a dark hall-way. A hooded figure disappeared into the wall . . .

With an effort I shook off the nightmare.

'Hang on a minute,' I said. I turned to Dad and told him of Wainwright's discovery.

'OK,' he said wearily. 'You win. I'll go and pack.'

I told Wainwright of our plans.

'You can stop the computer research now, we've found out what we want to know. Tell Ms Alexander what we're doing. We'll be staying somewhere near Borley; we can liaise through the local police if necessary.'

I heard a faint click as I was saying goodbye. Probably everything was being recorded automatically, I thought.

I put down the phone and turned to see Dad standing in the doorway. He looked hard at me. 'Taking charge, Matthew?'

I could see his feelings were hurt. I threw him a mock salute. 'You're still the Commanding General, Dad. I'm just trying to be a good assistant.'

He gave me a suspicious look. 'Sometimes I wonder just who's whose assistant round here . . .'

We did some hurried packing and then piled into Dad's pride and joy, a giant, red, off-road vehicle called a Kamikaze Land Tourer, and set off on the road to Essex.

The thought of visiting the remains of Borley Rectory filled me with dread, but faced with the idea of going mad like Backman, it seemed the only thing – terrifying as it was to do. I knew I just had to go there.

I was prepared to face unknown supernatural horrors when we arrived.

But I didn't expect someone to try to kill us on the way . . .

Chapter Four

AMBUSH

On the way down to Essex I gave Dad a potted history of the once-famous, or rather infamous, Borley Rectory.

It made quite a nice change – me lecturing him for once.

'Borley Rectory,' I began, 'was built in 1863 by a clerical gent called Reverend Henry Bull, as a home for himself and his family. Apparently an old monastery once stood on the same site – pretty significant, when you think of what went on later.'

Dad gave one of his sceptical sniffs. 'And exactly what did go on?'

'Practically everything,' I said. 'Please don't interrupt. I'll take questions later. Where was I? Oh yes, the rectory was enlarged in 1875; they built on an extra wing. By the time it was finished the place had thirty-five rooms.'

'Why did the reverend need such a big house?'

'Because he had such a big family. By that time he had seventeen children.'

I was about to make some crack about having to provide your own amusement in those days, when Dad beat me to it. 'The reverend gentleman seems to have been aptly named.'

Ignoring this, I went on, 'The trouble started almost at once. It was dragging footsteps at first, going past people's bedrooms at night. A maid heard them, then some of the reverend's daughters. One daughter heard mysterious raps on her door, another was slapped in the face by something invisible. A visitor reported books and clothes being chucked about in her room. One night all the bells in the house rang at once . . .'

'One moment, Matthew,' interrupted Dad. '*Seventeen* children, you said? Boys as well as girls?'

'I imagine so.'

'Bad, bored, mischievous little boys – who might think it a great joke to creep about at night, scaring their sisters and playing jokes on visitors?'

I shrugged. 'It's a possibility, I admit. But there's more.'

Dad sighed. 'I'm sure there is! Do go on.'

'People started hearing strange noises. The sound of rushing water. An invisible stagecoach going past the house. There were tappings and bangings, footsteps, crashing and wailing sounds, things flying through the air. There were various ghosts, a nun, a girl in white, a man in grey. Mysterious messages appeared on the walls asking for help, all the bells kept ringing, all the keys jumped out of their locks . . .

'This sort of thing went on long after Reverend Bull and his family had left. In fact, there were reports that the ghost of Reverend Henry himself was seen, not long after he died. Apparently he promised on his death-bed to come back and haunt the place! Anyway, later vicars had all kinds of trouble: noises, flying objects, things appearing and disappearing. Eventually the Church authorities decided the place wasn't really suitable for a rectory.'

Dad grunted. 'No wonder. Then what?'

'The place stood empty for years, until a psychic investigator called Harry Price took it up in the thirties. He rented it for a year and moved in a team of investigators.'

'Who found, no doubt, all the usual phenomena?'

I nodded. 'Price wrote a best-selling book about it. There were thuds, thumps, strange odours, mysterious lights, the smell of smoke without fire. Numerous ghosts and apparitions, all kinds of objects flying about. Some of the investigators held a seance and made contact with a ghost which threatened to burn down the rectory if they didn't leave. Which is exactly what happened eventually. Borley Rectory burned down in 1939.'

'A ghost of its word,' said Dad solemnly. 'Matthew, do you really believe all this nonsense?'

'Not all of it, no. Like you, I think those early manifestations might have had a lot to do with Reverend Bull's seventeen children – either through playing tricks or because they were triggering genuine poltergeist activity. It may well have been a mixture of both! The other spooky stuff could just have been imaginative additions to the legend. Later on, Harry Price was accused of faking things to boost the sales of his book.'

'There you are then. If the Borley Rectory

phenomenon is largely a fake, why are we hurtling towards it down this singularly unattractive stretch of road?'

We'd reached the stage in the journey where the last straggling edges of the outer-London suburbs were just beginning to merge into actual countryside. By now we were driving through desolate-looking fields broken up by a scattering of buildings.

It was a dull grey winter's day.

'We're hurtling because you always drive too fast,' I said. 'As to why we're going there at all, I didn't say I thought it was *all* a fake. It's always the same investigating the paranormal, Dad, you know that. You get legends and lies and fakery and self-delusion – but there's always the possibility of a little nugget of truth at the heart of it all.'

'So which bits do you believe in?'

'I think the poltergeist activity is too well documented to be a total fake,' I said. 'Especially all the really petty stuff. Bells ringing, keys leaping out of locks, books and bedclothes chucked about, bars of soap and candlesticks flying through the air. It's got the authentic pointless poltergeist feel about it.'

'So what's your theory?'

'You remember the business about ley lines we ran into at Stonehenge?'

Dad frowned. 'Mysterious lines of psychic power criss-crossing the country? Pure speculation, there's no actual scientific proof . . .'

'Maybe not. But two of the major ley lines intersect at Stonehenge, and we know some very strange things have happened there. Well, guess what?'

Dad has his faults, but no one could say he's slow-thinking. 'It's the same with Borley?'

I nodded. 'According to several sources it's almost as big a ley line intersection as Stonehenge.'

'And you think this has something to do with Borley Rectory's reputation?'

'Well, it's a distinct possibility, isn't it?' I argued. 'Take the more scientific theory about poltergeists – that they're not malicious ghosts or spirits but manifestations of telekinetic energy. If the rectory was built slap on top of a place of power, that might have the result of stimulating those effects. Particularly in some of Reverend

Bull's seventeen children. Tormented adolescents in a repressive Victorian society – it's a classic recipe for a poltergeist.'

'An interesting theory, Matthew,' said Dad. 'But it's all pure speculation. And what has it got to do with our present problems?'

I drew a deep breath. 'This is even more of a wild theory. It seems likely to me that someone who wants to manipulate the human mind might choose a place of power to do it in.'

'Perhaps. But how do we know that place is Borley?'

'We don't. But we've got two cross-references, remember. First, Doctor Backman and I both had the same nightmare.'

Dad sniffed. 'Pretty thin, considered as evidence . . .'

'Maybe. But there's also the fact that *all* the VIPs who had breakdowns had visited this part of the world immediately before.'

Dad nodded. 'That, I agree, is undoubtedly significant.' He gave me one of his rare smiles. 'And in the complete absence of any other theory, Matthew, we might as well pursue yours!'

I grinned back, pleased that my ideas had

passed Dad's scepticism test. I knew too that he wasn't nearly as unbelieving as he sounded. It's just his way to test any theory by arguing against it first.

We were well clear of London by now, driving along narrow, twisting country lanes. It was beginning to get dark, and to make matters worse there were patches of hovering mist as well.

Suddenly our unknown enemy struck.

The enemy was in the shape of a chunky black jeep – one of those aggressive-looking vehicles with bullbars all round.

It shot out of a sideroad, heading straight towards us. Dad stood on the power brakes and, to do it credit, the good old Kamikaze stopped almost dead. As a result the black jeep clipped the front of our bonnet, sending us slewing round.

'You stupid oaf!' yelled Dad.

He flung open his door, clearly about to get down and give the other driver the proverbial piece of his mind.

I saw the jeep go into rapid reverse and grabbed Dad's arm. 'That was no accident!' I shouted. 'They did it on purpose.'

'Nonsense, Matthew, you're just being

paranoid. It was simply a case of careless driving . . .'

'Take a look! They're about to have another go!'

Having backed away some distance down the sideroad, the black jeep stopped for a moment and then came zooming towards us again.

I could just see the hunched figure at the wheel, his face obscured by a pulled-up black scarf and a pulled-down black hat.

With a yell of alarm Dad slammed his door shut, threw the Kamikaze into gear and shot forwards.

This time the black jeep clipped our rear bumper, swinging us right round.

Straightening up, Dad set off down the narrow, misty road at top speed, with the black jeep close behind.

A sudden jolt, accompanied by a clang, made me realise it had caught up with us. The Kamikaze swerved wildly, but Dad managed to keep it on the road. He stepped on the accelerator and we surged forwards again.

The chase went on through the misty, winding lanes. From time to time there was another jolt and another clang as our determined pursuer slammed into our back bumper yet again.

Each time Dad managed to survive the impact, correcting the swerve and keeping going.

The black jeep was just as fast as our vehicle, but it was quite a bit lighter. Although it had the necessary speed to catch us up and ram us, it didn't have the weight to knock us off the road and force us to crash.

Because a crash was what our attacker was after, I thought. A nice convenient car crash on dangerous, misty roads. What could be more natural, more convincing? No doubt once we had crashed he'd finish us off by hand. He wouldn't want to use a gun – bullet wounds on our bodies would spoil the accident scenario.

For the very first time I was glad of Dad's colourful taste in transport. In any kind of ordinary car we wouldn't have had a chance. Only the sheer size and weight of the big red Kamikaze Land Tourer were enabling us to survive the repeated attacks.

I was proud of the old man's driving skills as well. Jaw clenched, white-knuckled hands gripping the wheel, he flung the big Land Cruiser along the narrow lanes like a real champion.

The road widened and the black jeep started to overtake us.

Dad swung the Kamikaze in front of our pursuer, there was another clang and the black jeep fell back.

It made several more attempts to pass, but Dad blocked each one.

I wondered how long the chase could go on. All we had to do, I thought, was to reach a village, or better still a little town. I'd pretty well lost track of where we were, but we'd be bound to reach *somewhere* soon.

Surely the presence of witnesses would put our pursuer off?

If we could last that long . . .

Suddenly the road widened again, and our enemy started to overtake.

'Don't let him get in front of us!' I shouted. 'He'll be able to block us off.'

I needn't have worried. Dad had it planned. It turned out to be his finest hour.

As the black jeep started to overtake he stood on the brakes again and the Kamikaze shuddered to a halt.

As the black jeep shot past, Dad threw the Land Tourer into gear, did a racing start and sped off after it.

Suddenly the black jeep wasn't chasing us any more. We were chasing the jeep!

My blood was up by now, and I wanted to give our unknown attacker some of his own medicine.

'Ram him, Dad!' I yelled.

'When it's time, Matthew,' he said calmly.

Dad chose his moment perfectly.

Waiting until the road swung sharply to the right, he sent the Kamikaze surging forwards. He rammed the black jeep on the bend, sending it crashing right off the road, through a hedge and into the ploughed field beyond.

Dad stopped the Kamikaze and we peered through the broken hedge into the dark and misty field. The black jeep was sitting somewhere near the middle. It had shot forwards for several metres and then come to a halt, thoroughly bogged down.

Dad opened the car door and started to get down. Once again I grabbed his arm. 'Where do you think you're going?'

'I want an explanation of what's been going on.'

'It's perfectly clear what's been going on!' I yelled. 'Someone's been trying to kill us! Now you're going off for a cosy chat with him in a nice dark field.'

'But he might be badly hurt, or even dead . . .'

'*We* might have been dead!'

'Come now, Matthew,' said Dad, always keen on the moral high ground. 'Common humanity demands . . .'

'Common humanity be blowed!' I peered into the field. 'Besides, he isn't dead. I can see him moving . . .'

A black-clad arm came out of the window of the jeep. Almost too late I realised that the black-gloved hand on the end held something squat and metallic.

I heaved Dad back into the driving seat, dived across and slammed his door shut – just as a bullet spanged into it.

'Well?' I yelled. 'Do you want to go and have a nice civilised chat about why he's shooting at us? Or shall we just get the hell out of here?'

As Dad considered, another bullet ricocheted

off the Kamikaze. 'Practically speaking, Matthew, your proposition has a certain amount of merit,' he said. 'We'll get the hell out of here!'

He put the Kamikaze in gear and we zoomed away.

Chapter Five

ALIEN ARRIVAL

We continued driving until we came to a village inn – I don't remember its name. At the time it didn't seem important.

Dad was so shaken that he pulled up and booked us straight in, without even checking the place out in the *Good Food Guide* or the *Good Hotel Guide*.

Fortunately we struck lucky. It was your classic country inn, with stone-flagged floors and low oak beams.

We went to our rooms for a bath and a change, and met again for dinner. The food was simple but good and Dad was even complimentary about the wine list.

Perhaps, like me, he was just glad to be alive.

I only hoped we could stay that way. The closer we got to Borley Rectory, the more frightened I was beginning to feel – as if something terrible was waiting for me there . . .

We'd decided in the car not to contact the police about our attacker and the car chase – it would have been too much red tape at this stage. We had coffee in armchairs in the lounge, looked at the maps we'd brought in from the car and worked out where we were. More by luck than judgement, we'd landed up not too far from the village of Borley – and whatever remained of Borley Rectory. We discussed our next move.

As far as I could see there was only one. We had to go and take a look at Borley Rectory.

'Tonight?' said Dad dubiously.

I shrugged, struggling to overcome my growing sense of dread. 'Believe me, Dad, I'm not looking forward to it, in fact I'm frightened witless, but I don't think we've got much time to hang around. I keep getting the feeling that things are coming to some sort of climax.'

After his recent experiences, Dad was in a more cautious mood. 'Oughtn't we to get in contact with Ms Alexander?'

'No!' I said quickly. 'That's the one thing we mustn't do.'

Dad looked amazed. 'Why ever not? Surely

after our recent experience it's obvious that we're dealing with enemy agents? And that sort of thing is outside our field. I have no intention of trying to be James Bond.'

'Don't be too sure about that,' I said. 'Just because we were attacked by a man in a black jeep instead of a flying saucer doesn't mean there isn't some kind of alien involvement in all this.'

'You mean they might be using human agents? Isn't that very unlikely?'

'They did it before, in the Stonehenge business. Remember Professor Mortimer, the old archaeologist who helped them? He was completely in their power.'

Obstinate as ever, Dad said, 'Ah, but he was a special case. They won him over by promising to reveal all the scientific secrets of Stonehenge, something he'd been totally obsessed with all his life. I might be tempted myself, if someone promised me all the hidden secrets of space. They'd find it a lot harder to recruit human agents for a disgusting scheme like this.'

'Maybe they don't exactly recruit,' I said slowly. 'Not in the way that you're thinking of, anyway.'

'What do you mean?'

'I'm not sure. I just have a feeling we haven't fathomed the real purpose of this scheme, let alone who's really behind it.'

'The purpose is obvious,' snapped Dad. 'To harm Britain by destroying the minds of its leading citizens. And as for who's behind it – take your pick. We may not be the world power we were, but we're not short of enemies.'

Dad's an old-fashioned patriot, and I didn't have the heart to tell him that we just weren't that important any more. It would only have started another argument.

'I think the plan is more ambitious than that,' I said. 'I told you before, I think this is only a pilot scheme, a try-out. If the ultimate aim is world conquest, then it's likely that the enemy comes from beyond this world.'

'I can see it's no use arguing with you,' said Dad. He's got this strange idea that I'm the obstinate one.

'Anyway,' he went on, 'you still haven't told me why we shouldn't call Ms Alexander and organise some help.'

'Because someone set up a very efficient

ambush for us on our way down here.'

'So?'

'They knew where we were heading for, worked out our route, and lay in wait at the best possible point.'

'I still don't see what you're getting at.'

'Wainwright and Ms Alexander were the only ones who knew where we were going,' I said simply.

There was a moment of silence while Dad considered this. 'Are you seriously suggesting that aliens have infiltrated the Secret Service? Do you really think Ms Alexander is a little green man – a little green woman, I should say – in disguise?'

I folded my arms and glared at him. 'I'm simply pointing out the logic of the situation. If you're not capable of appreciating it . . .'

Dad glared angrily back.

'That remark was quite uncalled-for, Matthew.'

'And so was yours,' I snapped. 'Who was it that said that attacking logic with mockery was the sign of a feeble mind?'

'Well, who was it?'

'You did!'

We sat eyeball to eyeball for a moment and then Dad laughed.

That's typical of the old man. Just when you think he's utterly unbearable, he suddenly turns human on you.

'All right, Matthew, I can see I shall have to humour you. I tell you what, we'll take a quick and cautious look at Borley Rectory tonight, just to see if there's any sign of unusual activity. We'll make another visit tomorrow morning and have a more thorough search. Then, whatever we find – or don't find – we'll contact the authorities. If you really don't trust Ms Alexander, we'll contact Chief Inspector Blane at the Special Branch and tell him your suspicions. Agreed?'

'Agreed,' I said. 'Sorry if I sounded rude.'

'Not at all,' said Dad generously. 'It's probably hereditary. I've been told I'm occasionally a little sharp-tongued myself.'

We grinned at each other, both relieved the quarrel was over. Then we went to find the land-lord and got precise directions for reaching Borley Rectory.

The landlord was a wiry old fellow with

white hair and a brown, wrinkled face, and he looked curiously at me when I asked for directions.

'Borley Rectory from here? Well now, I reckon you'd best go this way . . .'

He gave me directions and I wrote them down in my notebook.

'Long time since I've been asked directions to Borley Rectory,' he said. 'There's nothing to see there; it burned down before the war.'

I put away my notebook. 'Yes, I know. I hear it was quite famous for its ghosts once.'

'Most haunted house in England, they used to say.' He chuckled. 'Back in my old dad's time there was no end of visitors, journalists, ghost-hunters and that. That's all been quiet for years now – until recently, anyway.'

'What happened recently?' asked Dad.

The landlord looked uneasy. 'Oh, there've been a few tales. Strangers moving around the ruins, strange lights showing. Even lights in the sky, some say.'

'I haven't seen any reports,' I said. 'Nothing on TV or in the newspapers.'

'No one likes to talk about it much,' said the landlord. 'Borley folk have had enough of being pestered by outsiders.'

'I can understand that,' said Dad. 'Oh, what time do you lock the front door?'

'Round midnight.'

'Could I have a front door key then, please? It's just possible we'll be back late.'

The landlord felt under the bar, fished out a big, old-fashioned key with a hotel tag attached and handed it over.

'Right,' said Dad. 'We'll be off, then. Got those directions, Matthew?'

I nodded, tapping the pocket which held my notebook.

The landlord stared at us. 'Are you going to Borley Rectory now? Tonight? It'll be well dark by the time you get there.'

'That's right,' said Dad cheerfully. 'What better time to see a ghost?'

The landlord said, 'Just one moment if you don't mind, sir?' He produced a pad from under the bar, scribbled rapidly on it and held it out to us.

Dad looked down at it. 'What's this?'

'Your bill, sir. You'll oblige me by settling it right away. Just in case I don't see you tomorrow after all.'

Dad and I looked at each other and then back at the landlord.

'This is ridiculous,' said Dad. 'We're just going for a short drive, not disappearing off the face of the earth. We'll be back tonight, we'll go to bed, have breakfast, pay the bill in the usual way and then leave.'

'That's as may be, sir,' said the landlord. 'You must do as you please – when you've paid the bill. I don't want to spend weeks wrangling with some lawyer just to get my money.'

He held out the bill. 'Right away, if you please, sir!'

It was quite clear that he wasn't joking.

Indignantly Dad reached for his wallet.

'It seems Borley Rectory hasn't entirely lost its sinister reputation,' said Dad as we drove through the dark, winding lanes.

Ahead of us the mist swirled in our head-lights.

'That landlord certainly wasn't taking any chances,' I said. 'Still, you can't blame him. It takes a long time making a claim against some-one's estate, especially if they've vanished from the face of the earth.'

'I hope you're joking, Matthew,' said Dad severely.

'So do I,' I said, and shivered.

My sense of dread was growing stronger than ever. I felt we were on the verge of some horrifying event. I thought through my nightmares – was I going to go mad like the others?

I studied the landlord's directions with the help of my torch. 'I think we're nearly there,' I said. 'Let's park here and go the rest of the way on foot.'

'Is that necessary?' said Dad peevishly. He hates exercise.

'It's sensible,' I said. 'If there is anyone, or anything hanging around the ruins, we don't want to advertise our arrival with our headlights, do we?'

Muttering and grumbling, Dad parked the Land Tourer in the lay-by in front of a field gate.

We set off down the dark lane on foot.

Of course it never gets really dark, even in the country without street lights. Although it seems pitch dark at first, it's surprising how quickly your eyes adjust.

There was a fitful moon that kept disappearing behind dark clouds, and the white mist seemed to come and go, sometimes retreating, sometimes closing in on us.

It wasn't absolutely dark – but it was quite dark enough for me.

I shone my torch on an ancient, sideways-leaning sign. It read PUBLIC FOOTPATH in faded letters.

'According to the landlord, this path takes us to the Borley Rectory ruins,' I said.

We turned off the lane and set off down the footpath. It was narrow and overgrown and we had to go in single file. I had switched off the torch, not wanting to risk showing a light. I could hear Dad stumbling and cursing behind me.

I walked along, peering at the ground, trying to make out the bigger ruts and potholes and avoid them.

'I think we must be nearly there,' I whispered over my shoulder. 'Provided we're on the right path, that is!'

Suddenly I heard Dad gasp. He put a hand on my shoulder, bringing me to a halt. 'Oh, I think we're going the right way,' he said calmly.

'How do you know?'

'Try looking up, Matthew!'

I looked up into the night sky and then gasped as well.

Hovering in the sky was a glowing disc. The kind we had once seen over Stonehenge, the kind that had once abducted Dad. The kind used by the dark, hostile aliens who had planned to conquer Earth.

'It seems I owe you an apology, Matthew,' said Dad. His voice was a little unsteady – the sight of the disc must have brought back some horrifying memories. 'You were right about aliens being involved after all!'

As we watched, the saucer descended until it was hovering directly over the scattered ruins, illuminating them with its eerie light.

I shivered with sudden fear. In that moment, all my worst forebodings were justified.

The aliens had come to Borley Rectory . . .

Chapter Six

ALIEN POWER

As we watched, a beam of light shot out of the hovering disc to touch the ruins. For a moment it bathed the ruins in light, and then it disappeared. The disc shot up into the sky.

I looked at Dad. 'A transmission beam. Somebody's just arrived.'

'One of our alien friends, presumably.'

I shook my head. 'Unfortunately not. I think this is one of our alien enemies.'

There were two different types of aliens – two that we'd encountered, at least. The smaller, silvery aliens, the ones we'd met in Australia and later in the Bermuda Triangle, had been benevolent, or at least detached, harming nobody unless directly attacked.

The taller, black-clad ones, the kind we'd seen at Stonehenge, had been determined on conquest.

Dad and I looked at each other for a moment.

Then, without even discussing the matter, we moved forward cautiously.

Different as we were, Dad and I had at least one thing in common: we both suffered from insatiable curiosity. Whatever the danger, however afraid we might feel, we just *had* to know what was going on.

Leaving the footpath we moved forward across the uneven ground, heading for the ruins. As we got closer I could see a dot of light somewhere in the middle of them, a faint, unearthly glow.

Suddenly I tripped over something soft and bulky and fell headlong. I picked myself up and shone my torch on the obstacle.

It was a dead human body.

Shielding the torch with my hand, I played the beam along the body. It was a thickset man in a suit and a raincoat, nobody I'd ever seen before.

There was something huddled and shapeless about the corpse, something strange and unnatural.

Dad knelt by the body and lifted the dead man's arm. It flopped horribly, like a piece of overcooked spaghetti. I'd seen the effect before, in a body that had been found at Stonehenge. It was caused by a force-beam so powerful that it pulverised human bones. A force-beam that was the weapon of the dark aliens.

Suddenly a low voice growled, 'Don't move or you're dead.'

I shone my torch towards the voice and revealed a bulky figure in black, a big automatic in one black-gloved hand.

'Stop waving that torch about!' it hissed.

It was James Wainwright, the young agent who'd been bodyguarding the dead minister, the one man I'd told where we were going. Had our would-be assassin caught up with us?

I became aware of a smaller shape beside him. Ignoring his order, I swung the torch-beam on to Ms Alexander.

She too held an automatic.

I wondered if Dad's sarcastic remarks about aliens taking over the Secret Service had been all too true. Were both of them aliens in disguise? Would they suddenly shimmer and change shape? Or were they under alien control?

'I suspected there was a traitor in your organisation,' I said. 'But two . . .'

Another voice said, 'There's a traitor all right,

Matthew, but don't worry, it's neither of these two.'

I moved the torch-beam again and saw Chief Inspector Blane.

'Quite a reunion,' I said a little unsteadily. 'Who is the traitor, then? Where is he?'

Blane nodded towards the ruins of Borley Rectory and to the glow of light somewhere inside.

'Over there,' he said. 'We've got the whole place surrounded. Come on, you might as well be in at the death. And turn your torch off, for God's sake!'

I cut the beam and we all moved forward quietly. I was aware of other figures moving with us in the dark.

The light in the centre of the ruins was coming from a circular, open trapdoor set into the ground. Two figures stood by the circle of light, faintly illuminated by its glare.

One of them was one of the black-clad aliens I had encountered at Stonehenge.

The other was Harker, Ms Alexander's number two. He was talking in a low, angry voice.

'I brought the latest subject here but he tried

to escape. I had to kill him with the weapon you gave me.'

The alien made no obvious reply, but they must have been communicating in some way.

'Yes, of course I will find other subjects,' said Harker. 'But it isn't easy, it takes time. And you must improve the quality of your equipment. There are too many failures. They attract attention and endanger our successes. That fool Stirling and his wretched son are becoming a nuisance. I shall have to dispose of them – I tried this afternoon.'

I turned to Ms Alexander. 'What are you going to do?' I whispered.

'Arrest Harker and capture that – that thing,' she hissed. 'They can't escape, we've got the place surrounded with SAS men.'

'No, you mustn't,' I said. 'You can do what you like with Harker, but if you kill or even capture the alien there could be terrible retaliation.'

'Then what do you suggest we do?' whispered Blane fiercely.

'I'll talk to it for you,' I said. 'Keep Harker covered.'

I heard Dad say, 'No, Matthew!' but I was already running forward towards the two figures.

As I came closer to the open trapdoor I could see it opened on to something very like an operating theatre. There was a table and a complex array of alien equipment.

Both figures whirled round as I came forward and Harker reached inside his coat. There was a flat crack and dust spurted up at his feet.

'Don't move, Mr Harker,' I said. 'You're surrounded by armed men who are itching to kill you.' I turned to the alien. 'Don't you move either. You're in no immediate danger. I just want to talk to you.'

The alien stood motionless and impassive. I could feel no connection, just a blank wall of hostility and anger.

'I'm going to assume you can understand me if you choose to,' I said. 'If you can communicate with Harker, you can communicate with me. You tried to conquer Earth by invasion at Stonehenge and failed. Now you're trying infiltration, taking over influential humans. But you've failed again. The human mind is too complex for you to control. You only had a few successes like Harker here; the rest died or went mad. Now your scheme has been discovered. Your weapons may be superior but you're surrounded by human soldiers. Resist and you'll be shot to pieces.'

I picked up some kind of thought trace from the alien. Some kind of question . . .

It was asking what solution I was suggesting.

'Close down this experiment and leave,' I said. 'And don't try again. Your fellow extraterrestrials, the others who visit this planet, will be angry if you do. Just go!'

For a long moment the alien stood motionless. Then it whirled round a silvery device in its hand.

I heard a chorus of metallic clicks as weapons were cocked in the surrounding darkness.

'Don't shoot!' I called. 'Just wait!'

The alien pointed the device, not at me but at the open hatchway. The roomful of alien equipment exploded, sending up a pillar of flame.

As I jumped back I heard Harker scream. He suddenly collapsed, clawing at the back of his neck.

The glowing disc reappeared in the sky and a beam of light shot out, bathing the dark alien in its glow.

It looked at me impassively for a moment, the dark green eyes glowing. Then it raised a slender hand and disappeared.

The glowing disc shot upwards into the clouds.

It was over.

Except, of course, for the mopping-up.

The SAS went back to their barracks and the rest of us went back to the village inn, roused the astonished landlord and had a celebration.

Ms Alexander terrified him into providing drinks, hot and cold, and piles of sandwiches.

Then came the explanations.

Some time ago, Chief Inspector Blane had had the idea of covering *potential* VIP victims.

'Today it paid off,' he said. 'My men spotted Harker kidnapping one of our target VIPs and driving him away.' It appeared that this was the unfortunate man whose body I'd later fallen over.

'So what happened?' I asked.

Blane looked embarrassed. 'Somehow Harker realised he was under surveillance . . .'

'He was an experienced field-agent himself, remember,' said Ms Alexander.

Blane didn't seem much consoled. 'Somehow he managed to shake off my people in the London traffic and disappeared.'

During this period Harker had presumably taken his victim down to Borley, killed him when he tried to escape, and made his unsuccessful attempt to kill us as well.

He'd learned where we were going by bugging my call to Wainwright.

'Ms Alexander told me about your enquiry regarding Borley and about the link to Essex,' Blane continued. 'So we played a long shot, called in the SAS boys and surrounded the ruins of the rectory. That's when we spotted Harker again, when he returned for his rendezvous with the alien.'

Just as Chief Inspector Blane and Ms Alexander were about to pounce, I'd turned up and spoiled everything.

At least, that's how Ms Alexander seemed to feel.

'Had it not been for your doubtless well-meant intervention, Matthew, we might have captured a live alien and a room full of highly advanced alien equipment!'

'On the other hand,' I pointed out, 'you might very well have started an interplanetary war.'

'So what happens now?' asked Blane.

'Let's try to be optimistic,' said Dad. 'After two failures, two humiliating defeats, there's a good chance these particular aliens will decide to leave us alone . . .'

Some answers didn't emerge until much later.

The autopsy on Harker showed that he'd died when a minute neurotransmitter embedded in the back of his skull had malfunctioned.

In London a scattered handful of VIPs, the few successfully controlled like Harker, died at exactly the same moment.

As I'd suspected, the aliens hadn't been trying to destroy human minds but to control them.

Harker and others had lured victims to Borley where they were operated on with alien equipment. Most attempts at control failed. In those cases, when the neurotransmitters didn't work properly, they caused madness and some-times suicide – as with the minister.

Occasionally they also caused a random release of telekinetic energy, accounting for the random poltergeist effects.

Unlike Harker and those others who'd been

successfully controlled, the failed survivors, like Dr Backman, didn't die when the alien equipment blew up, perhaps because their transmitters had already malfunctioned.

Once the transmitters were surgically removed, most of the 'failures' made a full recovery.

Some mysteries were never really solved.

Dad raised one of them when we were talking things over at home some time later.

'Why did Dr Backman have nightmares about Borley Rectory and its ghosts?'

'According to Ms Alexander, Harker took a keen interest in the supernatural,' I said. 'It was a hobby with him. Apparently his flat was full of books about the subject, and he'd paid at least one ghost-hunting visit to Borley Rectory. Ms Alexander thinks that's when the aliens took him over.'

'That still doesn't explain . . .'

'Maybe Harker talked about Borley Rectory and its ghosts with Backman when he took him down there to be processed,' I said.

'I suppose it's a possibility.'

I grinned. 'Or maybe the ghosts are all real and they somehow got into Backman's mind while he was at the site of the rectory! Who knows?'

Dad still wasn't satisfied. 'And another thing,' he said. 'If, as you insist, you didn't pick up detailed information about Borley Rectory from earlier research, why did *you* have exactly the same Borley Rectory nightmare as Backman?'

'I've got an idea about that as well,' I told him. 'You won't like it.'

'Well?'

'I think the other aliens, the benevolent ones, put it in my mind as a warning, a clue to what was going on.'

Dad frowned, but he didn't comment on my theory. 'You took an appalling risk at the end there, Matthew,' he said severely. 'However, I suppose you meant it for the best . . . And it didn't turn out too badly.'

'Thanks a lot,' I said bitterly. 'Doctor Who and Flash Gordon get a lot more appreciation when they save the world!'

That's how it all ended – for the time being.

What really concerned me was how the dark aliens would react to their defeat.

Was Dad right? Would they feel that two failures were enough?

Or would they try again?

If they did, would the more benevolent aliens come to our aid?

Or would they stand back and leave us to fight alone?

Only time would tell . . .

If you would like more information about books available from Piccadilly Press and how to order them, please contact us at:

Piccadilly Press Ltd
5 Castle Road
London
NW1 8PR

Fax: 0171 267 4493